Fatou, fetch the water

Neil Griffiths

Illustrated by
Peggy Collins

In memory of Fatou Darboe,
who was both a wonderful person and teacher,
and to the special people of Gunjur in The Gambia.

Neil x

Red Robin BOOKS

Where story matters

Red Robin Books is an imprint of Corner To Learn Limited

Published by

Corner To Learn Limited

Willow Cottage ● 26 Purton Stoke

Swindon ● Wiltshire SN5 4JF ● UK

ISBN: 978-1-905434-16-9

First published in the UK 2010

Text © Neil Griffiths 2010

Illustrations © Peggy Collins 2010

Design by

David Rose

Printed in China

"Fatou,
fetch the water,"
called her mother from the house.
"We shall have
spicy rice for supper."

Fatou collected her large white bucket and hurried from the compound towards the well at the end of the village.

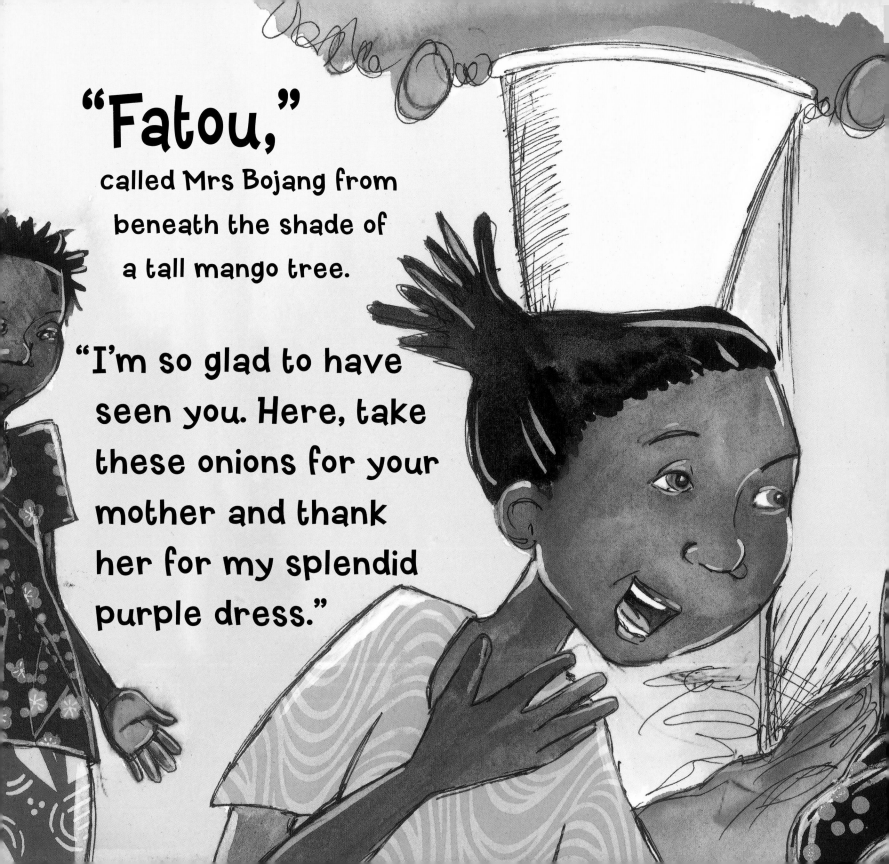

"**Fatou,**" called Mrs Bojang from beneath the shade of a tall mango tree.

"I'm so glad to have seen you. Here, take these onions for your mother and thank her for my splendid purple dress."

Fatou hurried on towards the well.

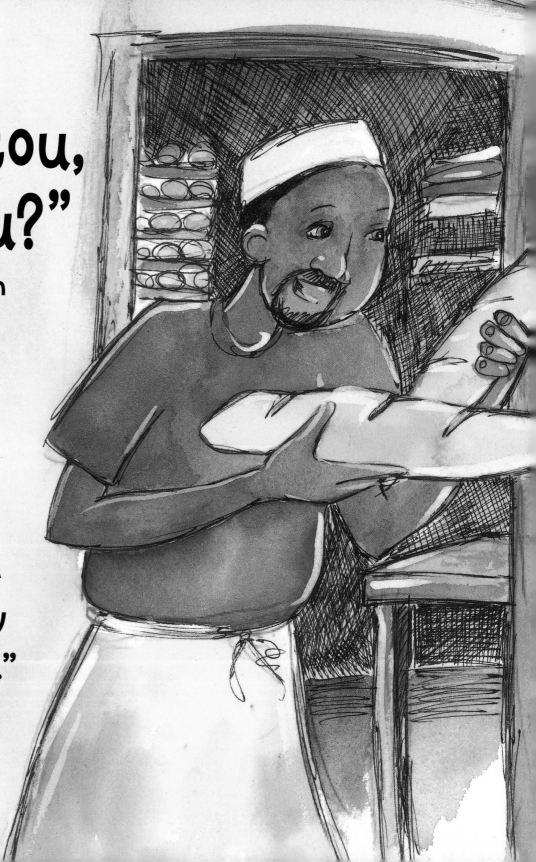

"Fatou, Fatou,
is that you?"
called Mr Jatta from
his hot bakery.

"Here, take some
warm bread to
your mother and
thank her for my
smart blue shirt."

Fatou hurried on towards the well.

"Fatou, waaaait,"
called Mrs Darboe who was busy sweeping her yard.

"Take these ripe bitter tomatoes and thank your mother for the beautiful pink shirt."

Fatou hurried on towards the well.

"Fatou, stop!"
called Mrs Samateh from the shadow of the wide baobab tree.

"Give your mother these newly-picked eggplants and thank her for the pretty yellow wrap for baby Mariama."

Fatou hurried on towards the well.

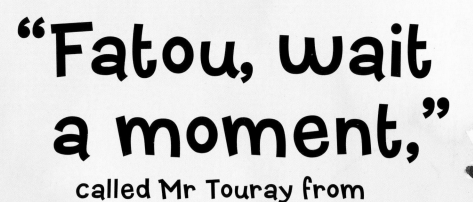

"Fatou, wait a moment,"

called Mr Touray from his busy bicycle shop.

"Here, give your mother these fine fish and thank her for my handsome green kaftan."

Fatou hurried
on towards
the well.

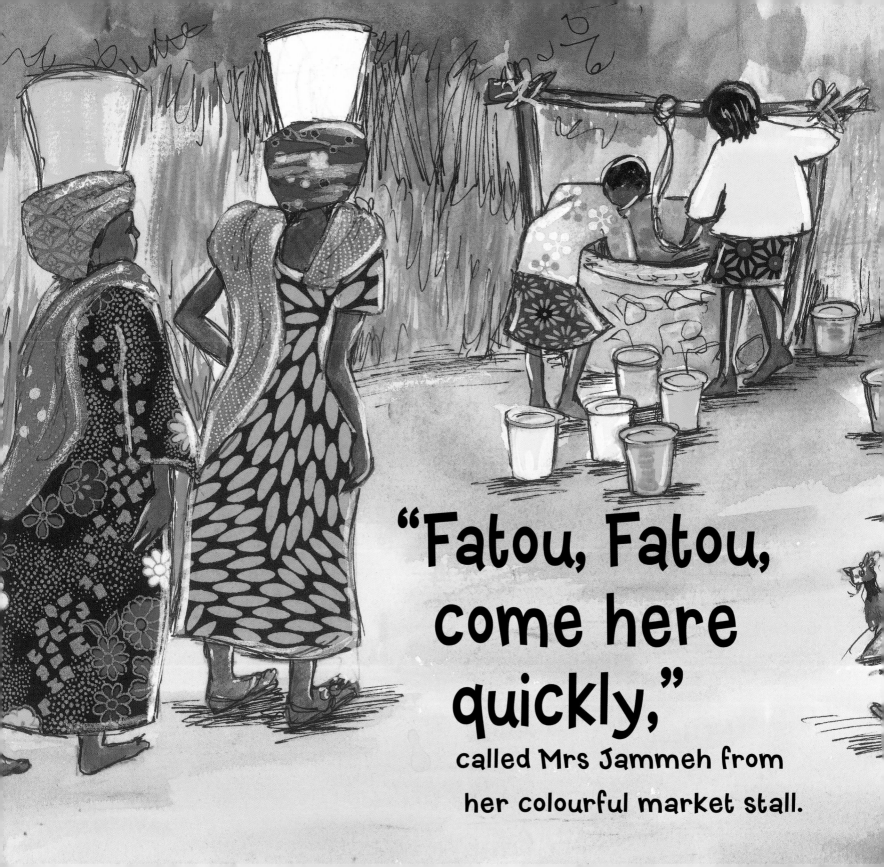

"Fatou, Fatou, come here quickly,"

called Mrs Jammeh from her colourful market stall.

"Here, take these dalasis and ask your mother to make me a red school uniform for Omar."

Fatou turned and hurried back home.

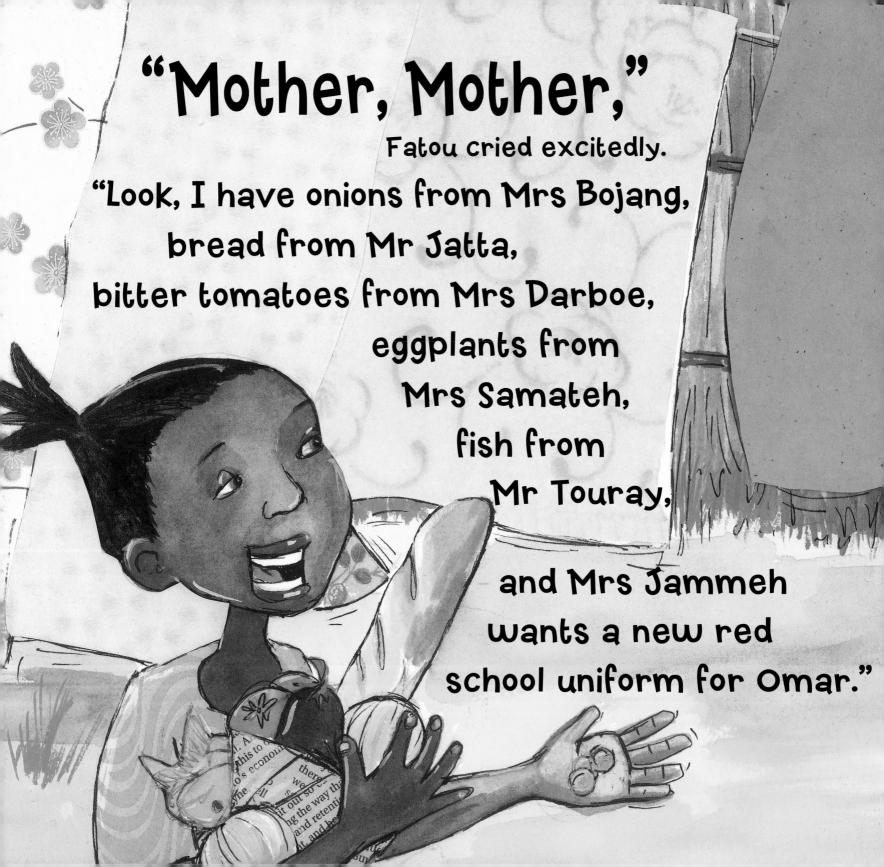

"**Mother, Mother,**" Fatou cried excitedly. "Look, I have onions from Mrs Bojang, bread from Mr Jatta, bitter tomatoes from Mrs Darboe, eggplants from Mrs Samateh, fish from Mr Touray, and Mrs Jammeh wants a new red school uniform for Omar."

"But where is the water?" asked her mother.

"Oh!" gasped Fatou.

"Here it is," called her sister, Isotu.

"I have fetched the water. You left the bucket at Mrs Jammeh's market stall," she giggled.

Later that warm evening, the family and the children's friends enjoyed an unexpected delicious feast.

Father was thirsty, but the bucket was empty!

"Fatou, fetch some w...,"

he began to say.

"Shall I get it?"

asked Isotu.

"No, I think it's
my turn, don't you?"

giggled Fatou.

The family
carried on eating
their meal, secretly
wondering what Fatou
might bring back home
with her this time!

The Gambia

Fatou's story is set in The Gambia, a country in Western Africa. It is the smallest country in mainland Africa and is bordered by Senegal to the north, east and south. It has a small coastline on the Atlantic Ocean to the west. It is named after the river Gambia that runs through it.

● The Gambia

Many Gambian men and women wear colourful traditional clothing that tends to be long and free-flowing to keep them cool in the heat. Women often wear a headdress like the one Mrs Bojang was wearing. It is called a musorr or tiko. The men often choose to wear a kaftan like the one Fatou's mother made for Mr Touray. It is a full-length, long-sleeved tunic. It is often called a fataro, jalabe or shabado.

The currency in The Gambia is called the dalasi. Mrs Jammeh paid for Omar's school uniform with dalasis. Notes come in denominations of 5, 10, 25, 50 and 100. Forty dalasis are equivalent to approximately 1 English pound.

Gambians love fish, which are caught fresh every day. One of the most popular is called Lady Fish. This is what Mr Touray gave Fatou.

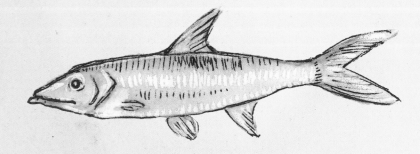